For information contact
R.Z. Enterprises of Florida
7640 Prospect Hill Circle
New Port Richey, FL 34654
www.rhymetimebob.com

Publisher's Cataloging-In-Publication Data
(Prepared by The Donohue Group, Inc.)

Hicks, Robert Z.
    Tommie Turtle's secret / Robert Z. Hicks ; illustrated by Ruthi Rolseth.

    p. : col. ill. ; cm.

    ISBN: 978-0-9792031-0-7

    1. Turtles--Juvenile fiction.   2. Friendship--Juvenile fiction.   3. Picture
books for children.   4. Turtles--Fiction.   5. Friendship--Fiction.   6. Stories
in rhyme.   I. Rolseth, Ruthi.   II. Title.

PZ8.3.H53 Tom 2007
[E]   2006940124

Typography: Publishing Professionals of Pasco, Inc.
Book Shepherd: Sylvia Hemmerly

Printed in China

TOMMIE TURTLE'S SECRET

Robert Z. Hicks, "Mr. Bob"

illustrated by Ruthi Rolseth

Little Tommie Turtle
is at home in his shell.

When he swims under water,
he swims very well.

When he's walking on land,
  his pace really slows,
    because he's carrying his house,
      everywhere he goes.

Tommie has a secret,
  and his secret is quite funny.
It's the story of the day he raced
  speedy Hoppy Bunny.

Hoppy Bunny was the fastest running rabbit in the patch.

He bragged about his speed, which no one else could match.

Tommie Turtle was out walking,
when Hoppy happened by.

Hoppy stopped to tease him,
no one there knew why.

"Hey, silly turtle,
  do you want to have a race?"

And then he stuck his tongue out,
  right in Tommie's face.

"Hoppy," said Tommie,
    "That was a mean thing to do.
If you really want to race me,
    then I **will** race with you."

"We'll start right here tomorrow,
    and this challenge I will make.
I'll race you to the big tall tree
    on the other side of the lake."

All the lake-land animals
gasped with much surprise!

"You can't win, Tommie Turtle!
Racing Hoppy is unwise."

"No," said Tommie Turtle,
   "He will learn a thing or two;
   that acting mean and bragging,
   is not the thing to do."

The race began next morning,
  just when the sky was light.
When the starter yelled, **"Get going!"**
  Hoppy ran right out of sight.

His friends moaned and left,
  when Tommie turned away.
They thought that Tommie knew,
  he couldn't win that day.

Tommie walked down to the lake,
and winked at Ollie Otter;
and then he swam across the lake
completely under water.

He swam as fast as he could swim,
and with no one there to see,
he raised his shell,
stretched out his legs,
and ran to the big tall tree.

Meanwhile, at the end of the lake,
Hoppy stopped to rest.

That turtle goes so slow, he thought,
I don't need to do my best.

Imagine Hoppy's big surprise,
when he finally reached the tree.

How the turtle got there,
was to him a mystery.

"Do you know what?"
    said Tommie to the bunny.
"The story of my beating you
    is really very funny.

But I won't say a word,
    or tell the folks I won,
        if you will stop your bragging,
        about how fast you run."

"If you'll be nice," said Tommie,
"I think that you will find,
you'll have a lot of friends,
and it's fun to be more kind."

So Hoppy quit his bragging,
  and the animals never knew,
    why he stopped his bragging,
      and stopped his teasing too.

Ollie knew what happened,
  but he didn't ever say;
    that Tommie was the winner,
      and won the race that day.

And Ollie Otter really likes

the way the story ends;

that Tommie Turtle and Hoppy

become the best of friends.

Ollie Otter's Thinking Questions

What is Tommie Turtle's secret?

Why do you think Hoppy was bragging about how fast he could run?

How do you think Tommie felt when Hoppy called him "silly" and stuck his tongue out at him? How would you feel?

Why did Tommie keep his winning the race a secret?

What did Tommie tell Hoppy to do to have a lot of friends?

How did Hoppy show that he could be nice?

Tommie Turtle's
Things to Remember

To make a friend, first be a friend.

You can't make yourself taller, by making others feel smaller. (Like Hoppy was trying to do by teasing Tommie)

Treat others the way you'd like others to treat you.

It's better to win a friend, than to win a race.

Being a friend means to care how others feel.

A true friend forgives even those who were mean.

Friends like to do things together.

Ollie Otter's Commentary

"Tommie sure is a smart turtle! He knew he did not have the physical makeup or speed to run on the ground to the tree across the lake and hope to win the race. Instead, he used his special abilities as a turtle to go faster. He knew that swimming well was his strength."

Have you discovered your special abilities and strengths?

"Tommie has a special gift of compassion for others. He wanted to help Hoppy learn how to be a friend, and to change his ways so all the animals could be his friends. Tommie forgave Hoppy for being mean, and gave him a chance to learn that it's better to win friends by being nice than by trying to beat everyone by running fast."

Is there anyone you can forgive for being mean to you?

"I think it was really special of Tommie to keep his winning the race a secret. Instead of bragging and seeking praise from the other animals for beating Hoppy, he chose to help Hoppy by not embarrassing him. That's true friendship!

Hoppy Bunny turned out to be a "winner" too. He realized Tommie was speaking the truth and trying to help him. After seeing the wisdom of Tommie's words, Hoppy changed from trying to be better than others, to being a friend to others."

Can you think of something nice you can do for someone to show friendship?

Bob laughed as he watched his wife Betty chase a green tree toad around the living room, trying to capture it under a paper cup. He started remembering his childhood experiences with wild critters on the farm.

Bob felt inspired to write a poem, and shared it with friends. Their enthusiastic response and encouragement to write more opened a floodgate of memories of all the animals and birds and critters he enjoyed when he was growing up . . . including a pet turtle.

"Tommie Turtle's Secret" was one of a set of poems that the staff at the 2005 Florida Christian Writer's Conference awarded "Best Submission for Children's Writing".

Robert Z. Hicks, "Mr. Bob," retired after teaching speech-communication for 24 years at the University of Hawaii. Bob and Betty currently live in New Port Richey, Florida.

Ruthi Rolseth is a professional artist who specializes in illustrations and murals for children. She especially likes to do art with an underlying scriptural theme. Ruthi shares a ministry with her husband Scott where she appears as Sunflower the Clown, and uses art as one of several teaching and entertainment tools.